PJ Library, a program of the Harold Grinspoon Foundation
67 Hunt Street, Suite 100
Agawam, MA 01001
U.S.A.

Designed by Michael Grinley

First Edition
10 9 8 7 6 5 4 3 2 1
072135.7K1/B1679/A6
Printed in China

: YITZI :

The Trusty Tractor

WRITTEN BY NAOMI SHULMAN

ILLUSTRATED BY SHELLEY COUVILLION

Farmer Sarah's veggies were delicious *and* nutritious. She always rode her trusty tractor, Yitzi. Together they did the hard, fun work of farming.

"I couldn't do it without my Trusty Yitzi," Sarah always said.

Yitzi wasn't just trusty. He was also a little musty and a little rusty.

But Sarah knew when to change his oil.

She knew how to handle his clutch.
She knew the right way to switch his gears.

"We're a great team," Sarah said.
"Rrrr," Yitzi answered.

Sarah and Yitzi did their hard, fun work every single day – except on Shabbat. Every Friday evening, Yitzi powered down his headlights just as Sarah was about to light candles. Then Sarah sipped a little grape juice as Yitzi sipped a little gasoline. Sarah munched challah as she sat on Yitzi's hood, and they both watched the darkening sky.

"Shabbat shalom," Sarah said, giving Yitzi a pat.

On Saturday, Sarah and Yitzi
picnicked under the trees and took
naps by the river. Sarah would read
books out loud to Yitzi.

When three stars appeared in the night sky,
Shabbat was over, and Sarah and Yitzi were
ready for another week of hard, fun work.

But as hard as they both worked, Sarah had trouble paying all of her bills. Eventually a very sad day came: Sarah couldn't afford Yitzi's gasoline. She knew what she had to do.

"I'm so sorry, Yitzi," Sarah said tearfully. "I'll make sure you go to a good home."

"Rrrr," Yitzi answered understandingly.

Sarah's neighbor, Farmer Ruthie, noticed the sign. She'd always wished her veggies could be as delicious and nutritious as Sarah's. Maybe Yitzi could help, she thought.

"I'm here to buy your tractor," she said.

"You have to change his oil every month," Sarah told Ruthie.

"I will," Ruthie agreed.

"And switch his gears slowly," Sarah said.

"I will," Ruthie agreed.

"And handle his clutch gently, the way I do," Sarah said.

"I'll do everything the way you do," Ruthie promised. Sarah knew Ruthie would give Yitzi a good home.

FOR SALE

Ruthie and Yitzi worked all week long in Ruthie's field, and Trusty Yitzi worked just as hard as ever.

Meanwhile, Sarah missed Yitzi and their hard, fun work. Yitzi missed Sarah, too.

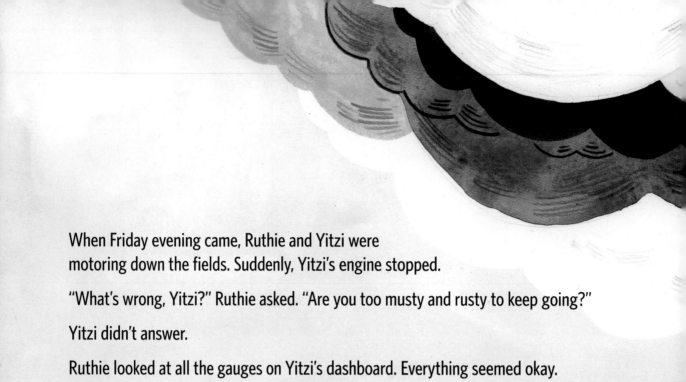

When Friday evening came, Ruthie and Yitzi were
motoring down the fields. Suddenly, Yitzi's engine stopped.

"What's wrong, Yitzi?" Ruthie asked. "Are you too musty and rusty to keep going?"

Yitzi didn't answer.

Ruthie looked at all the gauges on Yitzi's dashboard. Everything seemed okay.
"I don't get it, Yitzi," she said. "Why did you stop working?"

Yitzi still didn't answer. He powered down his headlights and rested all night.
And the next morning, Yitzi kept resting.

Ruthie marched across the field to Sarah's farm. "Your tractor isn't working," she
complained.

Worried, Sarah ran over to Ruthie's field.

But when Sarah got there, Yitzi looked fine – and very happy to see her! Sarah hugged Yitzi and then turned to Ruthie.

"I know what's going on," she said. "It's Shabbat."

"So?" demanded Ruthie.

"He's resting," Sarah explained. "That's what Yitzi and I do every Shabbat. He'll work even better for you tomorrow. You'll see."

Sure enough, Yitzi rested until Saturday night, when three stars appeared in the sky. Then his headlights popped back on.

"Rrrrr," he said, ready to start working again. And Ruthie found that he did, indeed, work even harder the next day. She also realized just how much Yitzi had been missing Sarah.

So Ruthie and Sarah decided they would share Trusty Yitzi. He worked in Ruthie's field one day and Sarah's the next. Then Sarah and Ruthie sold their delicious, nutritious veggies at the same table at the farmers market. When they worked together, the work was less hard and more fun, and now they could both pay their bills.

"We're a great team," Sarah and Ruthie said happily.

"Rrrr," Yitzi agreed.

And every Shabbat, the three of them rested...together.